UNDERSTANDING YOU

UNDERSTANDING RESPONSIBILITY

by Elizabeth Andrews

Cody Koala
An Imprint of Pop!
popbooksonline.com

abdobooks.com
Published by Pop!, a division of ABDO, PO Box 398166, Minneapolis, Minnesota 55439.

Printed in the United States of America, North Mankato, Minnesota

052022
092022

THIS BOOK CONTAINS RECYCLED MATERIALS

Cover Photo: Shutterstock Images
Interior Photos: Shutterstock Images

Editor: Grace Hansen
Series Designer: Victoria Bates

Library of Congress Control Number: 2021951851

Publisher's Cataloging-in-Publication Data

Names: Andrews, Elizabeth, author.
Title: Understanding responsibility / by Elizabeth Andrews
Description: Minneapolis, Minnesota : Pop, 2023 | Series: Understanding you | Includes online resources and index
Identifiers: ISBN 9781098242169 (lib. bdg.) | ISBN 9781098242862 (ebook)
Subjects: LCSH: Responsibility--Juvenile literature. | Accountability--Juvenile literature. | Social interaction--Juvenile literature. | Interpersonal relations--Juvenile literature.
Classification: DDC 152.4--dc23

Hello! My name is

Cody Koala

Pop open this book and you'll find QR codes like this one, loaded with information, so you can learn even more!

Scan this code* and others like it while you read, or visit the website below to make this book pop.

popbooksonline.com/responsibility

*Scanning QR codes requires a web-enabled smart device with a QR code reader app and a camera.

Table of Contents

Chapter 1
What Is Responsibility? 4

Chapter 2
Trust and Promises 8

Chapter 3
The Best Choice 12

Chapter 4
Taking Accountability. 16

Making Connections 22
Glossary 23
Index. 24
Online Resources 24

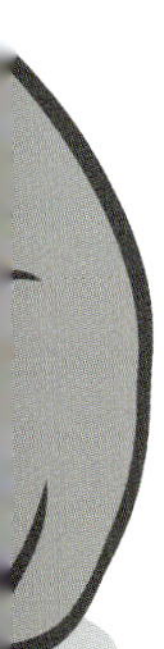

Chapter 1

What Is Responsibility?

Responsibility has to do with being a dependable person. To be responsible, a person must be **committed** to making good choices.

Choosing to save money for something you really want is a responsible choice.

Watch a video here!

Responsible actions can be simple things. Remembering to brush your teeth in the morning is an example. So is watering the garden during the summer.

Getting yourself to the bus stop on time is a responsible act.

Chapter 2

Trust and Promises

A responsible person keeps their promises. This makes them honest and trustworthy. Other people know they can count on them.

Learn more here!

Amelia promised her parents that when they got a dog she would be responsible for feeding it. Amelia feeds the dog before she leaves for school in the morning and again when she gets off the bus.

Chapter 3

The Best Choice

Responsible people will go out of their way to make good choices. They will pause and think about what they are going to do before they do it.

Explore links here!

Mason is outside playing with his friends on a Sunday afternoon. He wants to keep playing, but he chooses to go inside and do his chores. Mason knows his weekend chores need to be done before dinner.

Chapter 4

Taking Accountability

A responsible person takes **accountability** for their mistakes. They accept the **consequences** of their actions. They try to do better the next time.

Complete an activity here!

Parker got in trouble during school. He threw paper airplanes and interrupted his teacher.

He is not proud of the choices he made. He accepts the consequences and stays inside during recess.

A person does not have to perfect to be responsible. All people make mistakes and poor choices. Responsible people try their best everyday!

Recycling is a responsible action to take to protect nature.

Making Connections

Text-to-Self

What are some of your daily responsibilities? How do you remember to complete them?

Text-to-Text

Have you read any other books that talk about responsibilities? Did you learn anything different in those books?

Text-to-World

Do you think each person has a responsibility to the world? If so, give some examples.

Glossary

accountability – the quality of being accountable, especially willingness to accept responsibility for one's actions or choices.

committed – having made a pledge or promise.

consequence – the result of something.

recycle – to put through a process that allows used things to be reused.

Index

choices, 4, 12, 15, 19–20

chores, 15

consequences, 16, 19–20

mistakes, 16, 20

morning routine, 7, 11

pet care, 11

promises, 8, 11

Online Resources

popbooksonline.com

Thanks for reading this Cody Koala book!

Scan this code* and others like it in this book, or visit the website below to make this book pop!

popbooksonline.com/responsibility

*Scanning QR codes requires a web-enabled smart device with a QR code reader app and a camera.